The Sacrifice

ISBN: 1-4196-2753-8

To order additional copies, please contact us.
BookSurge, LLC
www.booksurge.com
1-866-308-6235
orders@booksurge.com

TODD
M. MORGAN

THE SACRIFICE

2006

The Sacrifice

TABLE OF CONTENTS

Chapter I, How did I get here?	1
Chapter II, The beginning	5
Chapter III, Computers and Girls	11
Chapter IV It's about Time	17
Chapter V, The beginning of a lifetime together	19
Chapter VI, Ready or Not	23
Chapter VII, A New (secret) Life	27
Chapter VIII, The Challenge of a lifetime	31
Chapter IX, Sometimes it is just good	33
Chapter X, All things Change	35
Chapter XI, The politicians don't always make good choices	41
Chapter XII, Some decisions are harder then others	47
Chapter XIII, Some choices you can never take back	51
Chapter XIV, WAR	55
Chapter XV, The first Heroes	59
Chapter XVI, War is Hell	63
Chapter XVII, One person can make a difference	65
Chapter XVIII, The light at the end of the tunnel	73
Chapter XIX, Ingenuity	77
Chapter XX, What price victory	81
Chapter XXI, All good things	89

In Everything I Have Done, I Have Only Been Able To Do What Others Have Supported Me In. My Wife Melissa Has Always Been My Sounding Board And Helped Me To Accomplish So Much By Just Being There. My Children, Nicolas May Never Know How Proud I Am Of Him Or Appreciate Being Able To Talk With Him. Jamie Has Always Been Someone I Can Kid With And Laugh With. Scott Has Such Youth And Vigor. Tessa Is The Baby Of The Family And Is Precious To All Of Us. Thank You All. I Dedicate This Story To My Family For Always Being Not Only The Place But Also The Warmth Of Home.

CHAPTER I
How did I get here?

How in the Hell did I get here?" Thought Patrick. The room was lit by one overhead light and had a single wooden table and three chairs. Green paint colored the wall and a single glass of water sat untouched on the table with the ice now almost completely melted. Patrick sat still, thinking of his life and the way it could have been. After all the time and blood he had spent doing what he thought was right, he still didn't know if it was right, but what did that matter now? Even if he was wrong, the past defied change.

After what seemed an eternity with only a few small movements of the clock his attorney finally walked through the door. The man walked to a seat and gazed down at Patrick, it was no secret that he didn't want to defend him or even deal with him but he had to, it was the law that even the worst of society would be defended. Patrick really didn't pay him much notice either. He was a tall man with a thin frame and a shaky voice. Not the ideal in lawyers, he didn't finish last in his class but nowhere near first either. No one in the world really wanted to defend him, and the firm chosen sent the most mediocre lawyer it had. They wouldn't be accused of sending their worst, but they would be damned if they would send their best. His voice finally made Patrick look up "Now Mr. Pierce, you understand this is only the judgment. If you are found guilty, then and only then will it be determined if you will face an execution. You do understand this don't you?" "Yes, we have been through this before. I have it." Patrick proclaimed with just a little irritation showing in his voice, he always seemed to have to repeat himself on everything and this was repeated so many times Patrick figured that he would dream about it or rather have nightmares about it.

The brown uniform of a Russian soldier stepped up from behind the door, "Mr. Pierce," he said in a heavily accented English, then turning to the lawyer, "sir, it is time." The soldier opened the door and let the two men out into the corridor. The corridor seemed much more dingy than before, it was really just the lighting though as one of the lights had burned out and hadn't been replaced yet. Patrick Pierce took the walk with forced determination; he could feel his breathing and the heavy thump of his heart. "You knew what the price would be; now let's just get this over with." He said softly to himself. The words granted no comfort and echoed hollowly through the corridor, the echo was only in his mind but seemed to hang in the air for an uncomfortable minute. His attorney and the soldier continued to walk down the hall without any idea of the thoughts that plagued their prisoners mind.

Patrick walked into the now familiar room, the American judge to his center, the Russian to his left, the British, French, and Chinese all behind the large oak table of the International Court. He moved to his spot, with all the television lights and cameras clicking, in the defendant's chair. The faces of everyone in the room looked stiff. The court was still except for a few whispered words. Patrick looked around for a friendly face and found only contempt at best and hate at worst. Even those that he could say he knew were of no comfort, for they looked on as betrayed friends or disapproving co-workers. Only the judges didn't radiate anger, and they expressed nothing in their words, actions or mannerism. The Judges had been informed, Patrick would use the word warned but whatever, that if they showed their contempt a mistrial could and probably would be declared. So they showed nothing for fear of spoiling the case and loosing their opportunity to be the ones to declare Patrick a traitor. Patrick figured he would rather have the truth than this pretense, but again this didn't matter. Patrick looked at each of the judges for a long moment and finally turned away, "I would hate to play poker with them" Patrick thought. Finally the American Judge shuffled some papers and then looked up. "All stand" came the load voice of the bailiff. Patrick slowly rose to his feet. The past was finally coming to him and deep in his soul he knew he had done the right thing, the only thing possible, but did it really change anything. Patrick hoped that it did or all this was in vain. Again the thought echoed threw his mind, "how in the hell did I get here?"

CHAPTER II
The Beginning

Patrick was born to an average family in Nebraska, in the United States of America. Growing up as many young boys, playing baseball with his dad and uncle was common and fun. He wasn't great at school, but never really had any problems. In the 3rd grade his life was shattered when his mom and dad announced they were divorcing. Like most young children, Patrick was devastated. For two weeks he stayed in his room and didn't play with his friends. Finally his father came to him, "son, we need to talk." Patrick was so lost at this time; all he could manage was a nod of his head. Tom Pierce looked at his son and picked him up, carried him to his car and put him in the passenger side. As they drove to the Dairy Queen for ice cream Patrick began to cry. Tom watched his son on that long lonely ride and wished he could undo this for his young man. When they reached the Dairy Queen Tom ordered a sundae with no nuts and extra chocolate. As Patrick finally started eating his ice cream, Tom took a deep breath. Slowly Tom began "son, I want you to know that me and your mom love you very much" Patrick interrupted "then how could you leave us, I know if you give me a chance I will behave better." Tom cut the youth off "son, son, oh my little guy, its not you." Tom leaned over the table for emphases "It was never you. You have been the best son a father could possibly want. I didn't leave you, but your mom and I couldn't live together anymore. We began to hate each other. I need you to understand that sometimes you have to sacrifice something in order to have something better." Patrick frowned for a moment then the young man asked with a rumpled brow "what is sacrifice?" Tom thought for a moment and then began; "it's when you're willing to loose something in order to get something hopefully better in the end." That was the first time Patrick ever remembered hearing the word sacrifice. It was a lesson he would remember for the rest of his life.

Patrick thought his mom looked great. The off white dress was long sleeved and as far as Patrick was concerned, the best wedding dress he had ever seen. He knew that she was happy, and at the tender age of 12 all he wanted was for her to be happy. After 3 years of struggling it was really nice to see her smile so much, besides Dale was a good guy too, he bought ice cream for minor things and played ball with him and his friends. The Wedding was by all accounts one of the best. There were no fights and the guests behaved for the most part.

The days flew by, Tom had been married a year and a half, but Patrick really didn't know Liz, his dad's wife, very well. They had gone off to Los Vegas to get married. Patrick found his father happy and with every other weekend they managed to build a good relationship. Liz seemed to make Tom happy, and the three of them took off on trips every now and again. Once they even went to the Grand Canyon. Things were going good in Patrick's young life. No one ever told him it all might end.

The knock on his bedroom door brought his head up from his homework. "Yes" Patrick replied. "Patty" his mom began, and then fell silent. "What's up mom?" Patrick asked as his mother walked slowly into the room. Patrick saw that something was wrong the instant his mother entered the room. Patrick now looked at his mother with all his attention, dreading what was about to be said and never expecting it to be as unbelievable as it was. "Pat, I'm sorry to have to tell you this but," she paused searching for the right word, and realized there were no right words so she closed her eyes and just said it. "Liz was in a car accident and" she stopped again trying to put off the words that she needed to say next. Knowing that he needed to hear the rest she opened her eyes to see Patrick's eyes burning into her pleading for the last part of the sentence, "Pat, she didn't make it." Pat just sat there looking at his mother. He couldn't believe what he was hearing. Patrick couldn't move, he could barely breathe. Then the realization struck him that his father would need him. "I have to go to dad." He stated as a matter of fact. Patrick's mom could only nod her head; she knew that he was right. For the next two months Patrick stayed with his father. Every night the crying coming from his father's bedroom would wake Patrick. The nights seemed to be the longest for Patrick and the crying was unbearable. Patrick would never let his father know that he heard him. Tom put on a good show during the day, but he was a broken man, even the time with Patrick seemed empty. Patrick didn't hear the crying that night and in the morning he slowly walked up to his father's room. "Dad, are you O.K.?" When there was no response Patrick hesitated and then stepped closer and opened the door. That's when he first saw the whiskey bottle. Tom looked up and smiled as he slurred "Pat, what's up?" Patrick looked down at his father and finally stated the obvious "Dad you're drunk." Tom made a face and shook his head; "Oh no, I just had a bit, come on over here." Tom stumbled and fell back to the floor. He remained still except for his breathing. That was the first time but soon Patrick found his father drinking at every opportunity. Patrick would spend hours taking care of his father. Nursing his dad became his after school activity. After Tom lost his driver's license, Patrick did the grocery shopping on his bike. The bills were soon being paid by Patrick or not at all. When Patrick began to talk about quitting school to help his father Patrick's mother became very concerned. She couldn't tell him not to care for his father but she couldn't let this go on either. Patrick could only say "Mom I know he hurts and I don't know how to help him, but I can't just let him be alone." Finally she came to Patrick with some papers and said "Patrick, have you ever heard of Alcoholics Anonymous?" Patrick responded "Yea, but I am not the one with the problem." "I am not so sure of that." She said as she handed the young man the pamphlets on AA. Patrick then learned from AA what an enabler was. Tom refused to go with him so Patrick found the courage to help his father in the one way he never dreamed he could. Patrick looked at his father, and even though he lay unconscious Patrick told him how he loved him too much to watch him do this to himself and when he was ready for help he would always be there. Patrick would sacrifice his father's care so his father could then get better. Patrick found it the hardest thing in the world a boy of 15 could ever do.

Patrick watched as his father eventually lost his house, his job, and his pride. One bright sunny day Patrick was walking home from school when his father stepped out from behind a tree, "Patty" his father pleaded through tears "please help me." Patrick looked at him and felt his heart beating hard in his chest. He had been building the courage to help his father for a long time and was able to finally say "I've been waiting for you dad. The first step is we need to go to AA" The first 3 meetings Tom held tight to Patrick's hand, walking though the door as a condemned man. When he regained his job after being sober for over 6 months he held a party, non-alcoholic. On Patrick's 16th birthday Tom came to his son "Pat, I know I could never have" he stopped and choked on his words, he looked to the sky and continued "thank you son."

CHAPTER III
Computers and Girls

The following year Patrick was introduced to two new things, one being girls and the second being computers. Girls came and went, all except Elizabeth. She lived two doors down the street and she wasn't considered a girl, she was a pal. Patrick never dated Elizabeth, or rather Beth. The first time he made out with a girl, it was Beth that he told first. When one or the other had some problem they always came to each other, especially problems with the other sex. The two became best friends and never dated each other; the thought just never crossed his minds.

With computers Patrick was a natural. The hardest programs came to him like he was born to it. Now Patrick thought that at least these things make sense, unlike most girls. Patrick was soon learning the hardware and the software. The computer was a tool that Patrick could get to do anything on. If a computer couldn't do something, Patrick could figure a way to get it to do it. The high school years flew by with Patrick receiving a full scholarship to collage.

The celebration for graduating from high school found Elizabeth and Patrick racing down a country road at 90 miles per hour together as they screamed at the top of their lungs in joy. When they stopped Beth turned and asked Pat "why don't you ever drink?" Patrick shrugged and then merely stated "my dad I guess." Beth knew about that and didn't ask further. The next question she found herself asking was "Pat, why" she fell silent and looked around, as if embarrassed to ask. There was nothing for miles. The two of them were sitting on a blanket about 20 feet from the car eating a picnic. She was glad to have graduated but frightened of the future, not that either of them would admit it though. "Why what, Beth?" Patrick finally asked. "Well" she fell silent again and found she couldn't say it. "Oh come on Beth we have been friends what, all our lives. You can ask me anything, you know that." Beth finally just blurted out "why haven't we ever gotten together?" The question struck him like a brick. It had never even crossed his mind, not even in a wet dream. She was, well she had always been his best friend bar none. He didn't think of her like that. "I don't know, I always thought of you as my pal." "Why?" Pat asked suddenly very seriously. This is one subject that never came up and for the first time in a long time Pat was uncomfortable talking to Beth. "Let's drop it ok." She heard herself saying even thought she had dreamt of Pat and she would never; never admit it, especially to him. Pat didn't know how to proceed even though he wanted to, so he heard himself saying "ok" as the subject turned quickly to other things.

The summer soon was ending and the good-byes exchanged as Patrick left for collage. Elizabeth couldn't afford to go away to college, so it was the local community college for her. Patrick had a full ride scholarship for his skill at the computer. At college Patrick found that computers were his passion, even the instructors realized his skill. He soon attracted the attention of the faculty for his expertise with them. Patrick found himself teaching the lower classes and acing his own courses. He also found that going home had new meaning as he looked for Beth. The conversation by the car began to haunt him. It took two years away at college before Patrick realized that it was Beth that he missed, even more then home. The day he was invited to go to FT. Lauderdale for spring break Patrick found himself unable to go if that meant not seeing Beth. The only way he could go was if Beth came too. Incredibly when he called her and asked she said yes right away. Patrick thought that was great, being how she said she didn't have anything else to do and she would be happy to go.

As Beth hung up the phone, she was all smiles. The thought of how she would tell her parents that she couldn't make the family reunion was not going to be easy. When her employer refused to give her the time off she didn't even hesitate to quite. She knew she could get her job back anyway, they couldn't keep good help and they knew it.

Ft. Lauderdale was as great as they say. Beth and Pat stayed in one hotel, of course only to save money. Pat didn't see anything wrong with that when Beth casually suggested it. The first day was a mess with the flight and just getting settled. By the first night they were ready to drop dead. As they walked into the room, Pat almost tripped when he realized there was only one bed. "Oh man, I didn't even think to make sure there were two single beds and not one big bed. Look I can sleep on the floor ok." Patrick said shaking his head feeling like a small boy that knew he was in trouble. "Pat, we have been friends for a long time and I think I can trust you, Kay" Beth responded. "Are you sure?" Pat said with a mischievous smile. Beth smiled back and cocked her head "hey; you may not be able to trust me." She responded. Pat, of course laughed. They slept together for the first time and never even touched each other. The second day was filled with sun, beach, and fun. Pat found himself getting mad when some guy from Texas started hitting on Beth. At first it didn't bother him but when a man asked her to dance and Beth stepped closer he found he was almost getting jealous. Pat couldn't tell but it sure did look like Beth was almost trying to get to him. Finally he had to walk over and cut in, asking to have the dance. Pat found he couldn't stop dancing with her, for some reason he just couldn't stand to see anyone else dance with her. For the first time around Beth, Pat felt his heart racing as he held her tight against him. Beth put her head down on his chest and they danced for almost 2 hours straight. The songs came and went and still they held each other. Pat had never forgotten the question of why they had never gotten together and now he could no longer answer, even to himself as he thought of Beth in ways he almost felt ashamed of as she moved her hands over his back. The smell of her perfume filled his nostrils and the feel of her silk dress next to him made him shudder. Patrick felt like a boy again. He actually felt relief when the dancing finally ended. He couldn't hide his attraction to her and wasn't even sure he could trust himself right now. Beth knew he longed for her and she could barely hold herself down but she made no mention of her feelings, she just danced. The dancing ended and they made their way back to the hotel at about 3 am. Beth raced to the bathroom and quickly shut the door. Pat sat down and turned on the TV. Beth came out of the bathroom in her pajamas and went straight to the bed, jumping in. Pat walked to the bathroom and brushed his teeth and put his pajamas on, the days events where still racing in his mind as he finished his nightly ritual. As he came out of the bathroom he found the room dark. "Are you going to bed or watching TV?" Beth asked him from the bed. "Oh bed defiantly." Patrick responded feeling completely exhausted. Pat shut off the bathroom light and slowly made his way across the dark room to the bed. As he laid his head down and rolled over away from Beth he casually said "and good night to you". The response of "no" from Beth made Pat roll over toward her. "What do you mean no?" Pat asked. Beth then rolled over to Pat, sliding close, looking so intently through the dark and moving even closer. Beth then leaned over and kissed Patrick passionately on the lips while moving herself on top of him, straddling him. Patrick then realized Beth was completely naked. He was already aroused, now he could barley breath. "I've wanted you for a very long time now, I don't want to be just your pal anymore Pat." Her breath was heavy, her hair hung down, and she could hear the pounding of her heart as she continued very softly, almost a whisper, "Love me." They embraced for the first time in a fit of passion. The night was filled with magic. Patrick reached up for her and pulled her close to him. He held her and kissed her so passionately it was as though she couldn't get close enough. The night proved to be longer than the day. As the convenience of room service was discovered, it made it too much for them to even leave the room, for the rest of their vacation.

CHAPTER IV
It's about Time

Nobody even batted an eye when they announced their engagement. The most common response was that it's about time; the two of them had finally seen what everyone else had for years. Patrick continued with collage and just before he earned his degree he looked into the military as a job. A friend of Patrick's, Tom, who had been in the military for four years, just shook his head. "Pat, you really are just, well, you're their property, but hey it's your call." Patrick's mom on the other hand turned pale and had to sit down. She knew better then to argue so she smiled and said "you will be careful won't you?" "Mom I haven't even signed. I just thought I would look." Beth had no problem. Her only comment was "you aren't going into the Navy are you, Tammy says her husband is never home, always, oh how did she put it. Oh yea, I remember "haze gray and under way." "I don't think I would join the Navy, at least not on the ships, maybe with the computers in port." Patrick responded. "Well, go look and we can decide." Beth finally said. As she smiled her stomach was doing summersaults, and when Patrick turned and walked away she exhaled a long slow breath and slowly shook her head.

Patrick came home with a long face. "Well I guess that makes it easy to decide. I am medically disqualified." Beth looked at him in shock "why?" "Well a Long time ago I was diagnosed with a sleep walking condition and even though I haven't done that in years I am still out."

Patrick then started looking in the civilian world of employment. He could make a lot more money, but he also found the really cutting edge technology rested with the government. At a job fair at college Patrick found a programming job with the federal government, The Defense Department. "We will have to move to Washington D.C." Patrick was explaining to Beth. Beth's first response was "could we wait until after the wedding?" Patrick smiled and replied "of course, love." Beth really was more worried about the Defense Department than she would say, but she knew he needed to be challenged and the Government was the only cutting edge technology that would really challenge him. The idea of working for that branch of the government though, kind of sent chills down her spine. It was a feeling she would never overcome.

CHAPTER V
The beginning of a lifetime together

The wedding was like a storybook; well maybe the book had a horror chapter or two but who's doesn't? The cake was late and Beth almost had a fit (Patrick made sure to stay clear of her until the cake did arrive). A bridesmaid's dress was torn from the store and of course it was too late to send it back for refitting and repair. Luckily Beth's grandmother was a good seamstress and had the dress fixed so well no one could tell that anything was ever wrong. Patrick's best man tried to leave him on a train bound for Chicago, all in good fun he swore to later, fortunately Patrick stumbled off just as the train was leaving. The DJ backed out 48 hours before the wedding, something about a fire. Talk about a scramble, but, as things seem to turn out, it happened that a friend of Patrick's knew a fellow who's brother played in a band, so they had a band for the wedding. It turned out that 3 months later one of the songs from the band took off and hit #1. They would be touring the country for some time to come. The song was recorded only because the date for one of Patrick's third cousins, who really wanted to go to the wedding more to see other relatives, worked for a record company and was truly impressed when she heard them. She then recruited them and the rest is as they say history. Of course no one ever believed Patrick when he told the story, everyone always had to ask Beth if it were true, then they would believe. Like so many weddings before and yet to come, when it came down to it, she was beautiful, and he was stunning, and they were happy. Even the cake did show up in time with just a little phone call that young children should not be allowed to hear.

Three weeks later they packed up an older ford truck with everything they owned and headed to Washington D.C. where Patrick would work at the Pentagon. Unknown to Patrick, one of his instructors had put in a good word for him or he would have never received the job. The only apartment that they could afford, and then just barely, was a one-bedroom crawl space tucked between and above stores. It really wasn't much and until Beth found some good used furniture in the paper, they ate off cardboard boxes. After each use the dishes were cleaned, there weren't enough dishes to have two meals off of without cleaning them anyway. The two found that grandma's wedding gift of pots, pans and dishes was more realistic than a lot of their friends, thank you grandma was heard often especially at meal times. Even so they smiled and went for walks in the parks, visited the monuments and Beth found a decent job just a mile and a half away, so she could walk or ride the old bike they found in the want adds to work, since they only had one vehicle. In 8 months they had saved enough to move into a new apartment and on the nights Patrick worked late, Beth would pour through the paper for a deal, there weren't many.

As Patrick came through the door with just a slight look of the long day he had, he suddenly noticed Beth standing in the doorway. She wore a short black lace edged dress. Patrick had last seen that on graduation and for some reason thought it was lost in the move. Then he saw the candles, as the smell of something cooking caught him and he felt as though he was melting in its aroma. Patrick had to close his eyes just to suck it in, in its entirety. Opening his eyes Patrick soaked up the sight of his wife and smiled; "so I take it we have a new apartment in mind." Beth shook her head up and down very slowly. "It's funny; I have some good news too. I was promoted today, it means a pay raise, can you believe it I now have a high security clearance, its way cool." Patrick then noticed Beth still standing there smiling. "I ah, the apartment isn't the big news is it, Love." Beth slowly shook her head "no it isn't" she said in a very slow voice that begged the question of what was next. "O.k. I'm all yours, what has you smiling from ear to ear?" "Pat, have you given any thought to," as she bit her lip and crinkled her nose she smiled again and continued "well, to names?" Patrick raised an eyebrow "names, like little persons names?" He asked in a voice that slowly rose in pitch as his eyes went wide, his arms limp, and his heart started thudding through his chest. Beth slowly shook her head up and down "yes!" Patrick leapt to her and picking her up off the ground, he then kissed her long and passionately.

CHAPTER VI
Ready or Not

Beth woke up at 12:30 am and slowly walked downstairs so Patrick could get some more sleep, if this was the time he would need it, and if not he would still be going to work in the morning. She timed the contractions for three and a half-hours. She then went back upstairs and turned on the light as Patrick slept, "I think I lost my mucus plug." She stated matter-of-factly." Pat sat up and looked at his wife. "Is it time?" He asked since he really didn't know what a mucus plug was or what that meant. Beth was already on the phone to the doctor. As she hung up, "no, not yet." She stated. Beth then went back to the bedroom door and shut off the light as she went back to the living room. Pat sat there for a few minutes, his heart pounding and his thoughts racing. "O.K. I am not going back to sleep." Patrick thought. At this he got up and went to the shower, it may be the only chance he had to get ready for what seemed to be a most important day ahead. By 4:30 am Beth was having contractions every five minutes. Pat was just now getting dressed when Beth walked in, "it is now time." The drive to the hospital went well, so Pat thought; only one red light was missed. The hospital staff sent them to the maternity wing and once there they were told that today was the day.

As labor began to be more intense, Pat looked at his wife in awe. The contractions dried out her mouth and Pat quickly provided ice chips. Thankful that he could do something other then stand there and say "breath". He really couldn't blame her if she did reach up and smack him, he felt like doing the same thing to himself as she went through this intense pain breathing in short breaths and him standing there encouraging her to "breath". The ice chips gave him something useful to do. The doctor took position and Beth began bearing down. Pat looked at the doctor getting his tools ready and thought "shouldn't you be looking at Beth?" but he said nothing. As Beth screamed in pain Patrick looked at her trying to give some comfort. Then, as if by magic, a small head came out of his wife. The doctor suctioned the mouth, and the head, still not all the way out of his mother, began to scream. The sound was like nothing Patrick ever even dreamed. The sight was unbelievable really, a head protruding from his wife screaming and red, it just didn't look right. He stood looking at the head as a shoulder and then one arm became visible. The second shoulder then emerged with an arm attached to it. After the second arm came out, the whole child just slid right out. Patrick found himself breathing hard even though he had done nothing. "Patrick would you like to cut the cord?" the doctor asked. Patrick could only shake his head up and down as words failed him at the moment. Patrick's hand shook slightly as he cut the cord still feeling as though he had just witnessed a miracle. The small child was brought to another area of the room and Patrick stood transfixed, looking first to Beth then to the child until Beth looked up at him and finally told him, "Go see your son." Patrick needed no further encouragement as he walked to his newborn son. Patrick would never be able to tell anyone what this felt like, no words would ever be able to describe what he felt or dreamed that moment. The Doctor and nurse cleaned and checked the small boy that Patrick stared at not realizing his jaw stood open, and not caring if he had realized it anyway. The moment was too much to concern oneself with such trivial matters.

Joshua was born healthy and loudly. He liked to see if both mom and dad could live with little to no sleep. Most of the time he succeeded in his attempt to find out how long they could go before they had to find sleep. Patrick was pleased that he only stumbled twice while rocking Joshua at 3-5 am with his eyes closed. Neither Patrick nor Beth could ever tell you how they survived, but they did. Diapers, crying, puking up, and still all the boy ever had to do was smile and he had everyone wrapped around his little finger. Patrick spent more time at home and still excelled. At work he was fast becoming the most talented program and operations specialist in the defense department. Patrick also found that he could work himself to death and the only one that would ensure he leave on time was himself. With Beth never bickering, she would just tell him what he missed out of Joshua's life for that day.

Patrick began to be his own advocate. He shut off his computer when he was due to go, and even though he brushed past a few of his supervisors, they would not stop him, he was too good. When Patrick was passed up for promotion, he calmly walked into John Fritz's office. "John, I see you didn't think I deserved an advancement." Patrick stated calmly. John looked up from his desk "Well Patrick," he began "you don't go overboard for the department." Seeing Patrick's face John continued "Well Patrick what did you expect? You never stay over and to ask you to come in on the weekend is out of the question. You just don't put in that little extra needed push." Patrick started slowly in a low strong voice "John, you know, even though I leave on time every day, I get twice as much work done as anyone else in this department. I am not going to go through what you already know though, so here it is in a nutshell, either I am promoted as I should be or consider this my two weeks notice." Patrick didn't even bother to look back to listen to Johns "buts" come pouring out of him; Patrick just turned and walked to his desk. John continued to call after him though "Patrick, Patrick come on now, hey wait-a-minute," as John got up from his desk and ran after him. "Come on, you can't mean that, you have 10 years with the government, your not just going to throw that away!" Patrick stopped and turned to face John "John I have three job offers in my desk that would double my salary or even triple it right now, with better medical and a better retirement option. I am not a pushy person but I will not allow myself to be drop kicked for not staying after hours. Do not misinterpret quiet for complacent or polite for a pushover. You have two weeks before I leave, either you correct this problem or I am gone." There was no anger in his voice; he just simply stated what he was going to do. That made John even more worried. Even though Patrick never stayed after, he still carried the department, and everyone knew it. Patrick would get his promotion, because everyone in the whole damned pentagon knew Patrick by reputation alone, and he would be a valuable asset anywhere.

CHAPTER VII
A New (secret) Life

Colonel Neil looked at the paper in front of him and smiled. Finally Patrick was going to be made available to him through the promotion process. "He will be coming to us "Neil stated to no one in particular as he closed Patrick's file. After a few minutes he looked up and called his receptionist into his office, "Would you please make the standard arrangements for the acquisition of a new hire". "Of course Colonel." She stated as she began the necessary process.

John Fritz had been in the pentagon for a long time, but he had never received a letter like this, so he walked it over to Patrick's office, knocked once and opened the door. "Well Patrick, you have been offered a promotion." He stopped for effect, "if you want this one." Patrick looked up from his desk with a cock from his head, "why wouldn't I?" Patrick asked with a smile. "Well" John started "this letter is supposed to tell you the what's and where's of the position being offered." John stopped at this and just looked at the paper. "O.K. let me know what I'm in for already." Patrick could sense John's apprehension. Again John looked at the paper; finally he began to read, "Position, classified. Supervisor, classified. Location, classified. Pay, classified. Requirements, classified. Duration, classified." John raised his arm's and shrugged "the only thing this letter says is tomorrow at 2pm you will be instructed to an office via your line" nodding towards Patrick's phone, "6799 for a briefing." John looked up, seeing utter bewilderment on Patrick's face. "Congratulations on your promotion, ha ha ha" John couldn't and didn't really want to contain his laughter as he put the letter down in front of Patrick and walked out laughing all the harder. Patrick sat there for a long time. "Black box bullshit," Patrick thought, "oh shit", they were the worst to work for, with, or around. Patrick had to smile though. What's the worst that could happen? The position is ranked as a promotion so he would at the very least receive a pay raise. He would go and find out what it's all about anyway, the truth be told Patrick always liked mysteries and this was the first he had been a part of so he wouldn't miss it for the world.

As Patrick walked through the front door, Beth came to greet him. "Hi, any word on when we go on vacation or are we looking for work?" she said with a smile. Joshua came running "dad" he screamed with a big hug from such a little guy. "Mom said we are having tacos for dinner." Patrick smiled "that sounds great." And with that Patrick went off to help the little boy build his Lego empire or ship, he couldn't remember which and really it didn't matter as long as the two of them would build it together.

Later that night, as Patrick explained the "promotion" to Beth, she could feel the old shiver run down her back. "Well, we do want to move before Joshua goes to the junior high, so if it's a good job, why don't we go for it." Patrick just smiled, he knew that would be her answer and he already knew that he would have to say yes, it felt too much like a challenge, so much so that he just couldn't let it go.

2pm promptly, Patrick's phone began to ring. As Patrick answered he heard "they're late!" as John screamed into his ear. The laughter was louder then it should have been. Patrick looked across the room to John and slammed the phone down.

Patrick's heart was pounding hard when the phone rang again, Patrick hesitated and finding John nowhere near a phone, he then lifted the receiver. "Hello." Patrick said. The instructions were very specific, 9am tomorrow at an office across town they would be expecting him and he has an administrative day off. Well, thought Patrick, it's better than a day here and if they are done early he can meet Beth for lunch, sounded good no matter what.

9 am, and Patrick stood outside of an office that was nothing fancy, just one of a row of offices. Patrick licked his lips and then wiped them dry with his hand, took a deep breath and opened the door and stepped inside. The receptionist seemed nice. "Hello, Patrick?" As Patrick nodded "I'm Shannon; Colonel Neil is expecting you." She smiled and motioned to a door behind her. Patrick tried to smile back but it was painfully obvious that he did not feel like smiling, only leaving and never looking back. "Well" thought Patrick, "what will it be?" He walked toward the door Shannon had indicated and opening it, stepped through. Colonel Neil sat behind a simple metal desk; to either side of Patrick stood an armed guard. As Patrick shut the door behind him, Colonel Neil spoke "everything, and I mean everything you hear, see, or even dream is not to be spoken of or told to anyone, including your wife." The two armed guards then very forcefully and deliberately pulled the slides of their pistols and locked a bullet in place. "Do I make myself clear?" Colonel Neil asked. "Crystal" was all Patrick could manage at the time. "Good, either you're in or not you get a pay raise to level 22 and you and your family move, I need a yes or no right now before I can tell you any more." Patrick stood still for a moment, looking to his right he could see the soldier holding the pistol up. Patrick looked back to the colonel, "all right, I'm in.'

"O.K." The Colonel began "you two" indicating the two soldiers "are dismissed". As the soldiers left the Colonel looked at Patrick, "They don't have a high enough security clearance" he explained to Patrick. "Your security clearance is as of now" as he stamped a piece of paper with Patrick's Department of Defense picture on it, "is equal to the President of the United States of America." Colonel Neil stopped to let that soak in. "your new home will be in New Mexico; I will finish briefing you at site 2." Colonel Neil handed Patrick some papers. These will provide for your move and get you in a house, after you're there phone this number." Pointing to a phone number in red. "You have one month of vacation and move time, I look forward to seeing you there, Patrick." Patrick looked at Neil "OK can you tell me anything about the job?" Colonel Neil's head popped up "no, not now." With a nonchalant calm which also ended the conversation.

One month later, Beth, Joshua, and Patrick finally moved in to a beautiful house in a quite suburb in New Mexico. Hot was all Patrick could think. The next day, he would again meet Colonel Neil and he would admit only to Elizabeth that he was a bit apprehensive. Beth just listened, she always felt apprehensive about the military, and all this secrecy was, well it just annoyed her. "It seems like a good move so far." She stated. "Hey, you're right; I would still like to know what I am going to be doing though." Pat said as he looked out the window.

CHAPTER VIII
The Challenge of a lifetime

As Patrick walked into the two-story building he could just wrinkle his nose. "This place looks like a World War II building that should have been bulldozed a long time ago; I hope this isn't the whole thing." Patrick thought to himself. Inside were two visible guards and an elevator. Patrick just shook his head. "This is code breakers," he thought as he cursed himself for taking this job. "The most boring job in the universe" Patrick forced a smile as Colonel Neil came out of a side office. "Hello Patrick," Exhaling visibly he began "there is so much to do today and today is going to be one of those days were your overloaded. Don't let it throw you." Motioning to the Elevator "shall we?" A faint smile on his lips, almost to say "check this out." The smile wasn't lost on Patrick, who slowly stepped in the elevator. Colonel Neil took out an electronic key card, inserted it and punched a code. "Ready?" Neil smiled even more as he looked at Patrick. Patrick shook his head slowly, yes as the door shut. The feel of the elevator going down caught him off guard; he hadn't expected to go down. "How far down?" Patrick asked. Neil looked at him "just about 9 levels. Only the last level has anything, the rest are just part of a maze so no one finds us."

Colonel Neil slumped down and looked at Patrick as the elevator continued down, "I am assuming you have heard of Roswell, right." Patrick looked at Neil and cocked his head

"What, the aliens?" Patrick could hear his own cynicism, which quickly faded as Colonel Neil continued "yep, that's it, but the aliens didn't crash. They were shot down, and not by us." He paused to let his statement sink in, and then he continued. "The Nyktarians came here to warn us and help us. The Chiria, well they don't want them to help us. You see they are antagonists, but neither will risk an open fight. An open fight would be too devastating, so, anyway, the Chiria began looking for a cheap energy source, which they found in our asteroid belt. The Nyktarians don't want them to have it and since we are the closest enslave able race, neither do we." Patrick just stared; a bit of shock had set in. The elevator doors opened to a large room with a few offices in the corner and a massive computer system with a dozen counsels. Neil continued as he stepped out of the elevator, "seems one of the technologies the Chiria have is the ability to open a wormhole from one point in the universe directly to another point." Spinning around to face Patrick, 'pretty cool huh." Neil continued towards the offices "the Nyktarians gave us some hardware to collapse these wormholes before they open, and that's your job, collapsing those wormholes before Chiria shock troops come pouring through to chew us up and spit us out." Patrick followed Neil into his office, letting the enormity of this filter into his head. "Oh my God." Was all he could finally say as his face went pale. Neil just smirked. "I knew you would understand."

CHAPTER IX
Sometimes it is just good

The next seven years saw the perfect life, Joshua grew, Beth loved their home and Pat never had to work late. Most of all Patrick believed in his work, he knew it was important. Patrick learned everything he could about the alien technology, while also working his way up to chief civilian at the site. Colonel Neil and his wife, Amy, and his two sons became good friends, almost like family, so when Patrick arrived at the complex to hear the security officers ask if he had heard that Colonel Neil was leaving. Patrick felt as though he had been kicked. The long elevator ride seemed even longer as he realized how much he would miss his friend. When the doors opened, a Party like atmosphere greeted him, with Colonel Neil as the man of the hour. As Colonel Andrew Neil waved him over Pat could tell it was serious. Stepping into his office, Colonel Neil closed the door, "what's up Andy?" Patrick asked. "You know I am being transfered, right?" "I just heard, you know you will be missed." Pat put on a faint smile for his friend, but he didn't feel like smiling. "Maybe not," Patrick was taken back as he listened to his friend. "You see I am being promoted to General and taking direct command of site #1. "I will be in overall command of ops." He said proudly. Neil paused for effect and then continued "am bringing you with me." It was a statement but also a question. "You want a promotion Pat?" Patrick looked at him and shook his head up and down finally managed "oh yea." "Good" Neil said as he grabbed Pats hand and slapped him on the back as hard as he could "we are moving to the Rockies, in California my boy!" With that Patrick became chief civilian on the entire project, with a substantial pay-raise.

The move went smoothly, except of course Joshua didn't like moving schools in junior high. The making of new friends was, well just odd.

The new site was in king's canyon and dug a bit deeper than site 2. After three years, Patrick was well liked in the community, had a good working relationship and knew more then anyone about the alien technology. Life was very good, and about to be made a lot more complicated.

CHAPTER X
All things Change

At 4 am on Tuesday, site one was operating normally when a technician named John looked at the screen, "We have one." He stated calmly as he yawned just as a wormhole began to form. Punching in the coordinates he pressed the button and looked for the signs that the wormhole was collapsing, only to find nothing. John checked his instrument again and reinitiated, still nothing. John was now sitting up in his chair when the fire alarm sounded. The collapsing mechanism was smoking. "Oh my God!" John screamed racing to a yellow phone as a Sergeant took a fire extinguisher to the smoking piece of equipment. "This is site one, we are off line, site two emergency initiate shutdown, this is not a drill, I say again this is not a drill." The person on the other end of the line must have been screaming for John to pull the phone away from his ear so quickly. After a long tense 20 seconds where the world seemed to be breathless, the wormhole finally began to collapse. "That leaves only one working site." John stated to no one in particular and to everyone. John then called Patrick as the sergeant called the general. It was going to be along night.

"Andy." General Neil looked up at Patrick. "I think I can duplicate the collapsing mechanism." Now Neil did stop. "That's never been done before." Andy was saying. "Well I think I can, and, with your permission, I would like to try."

Neil sat silently before slowly nodding. "Go for it Pat, just keep me informed." Patrick had already run some tests, but now he went full tilt. In four months Patrick brought a prototype into General Neil's office. "I think this will work and we can run it here with site 2 as a backup in case of a problem, OK." Neil looked at the gadget, he never really liked computers, he knew what he had to and that was it. The internals were completely foreign to him. Well it looked cool anyway. "We can install and test it in 4 hours, so next week we can give it a try." Patrick was saying. "I don't mind telling you this makes me uneasy. The technology is something we don't fully understand and well the thought of a really big bang does come to mind." Neil said as he looked at the small machine. "Well we don't have anything to loose but our lives." Patrick said. With a slight half hearted laugh Neil looked at his friend and shrugged "you're right, lets set it up."

On Sunday, Patrick was at the mall when his beeper sounded. As Patrick phoned the base he expected a simple problem, what greeted him was panic. "Sir, I will transfer you now." Patrick just smiled at Beth, wondering what this was all about. "Pat" Neil almost screamed. "Site two just went down." His heart felt like it skipped a beat "How long do we have?" Patrick asked. "32 minutes." Patrick looked at his watch "the prototype." "It's our only option." Neil responded. "I can't make it there in time." Patrick looked around as though he might find something. "Yes you can, we have full authority of the president himself, where are you?" "At the mall." Patrick responded. "OK I am having you picked up. What do we need to do to finish installing this thing?" Patrick looked at his watch as he began speaking "OK I can run you through it but I can't get there in time." Neil responded in a stern voice "An Apache helicopter is en-route to you; you will make it here OK." Patrick realized that Neil was right and simply said "Fine." as he started to explain the procedure to hook up the prototype, there would be no time for any testing though.

The captain couldn't believe it, here he was being ordered to land in the middle of a mall with a fully loaded apache. "No. You are to lose your load captain." Came the voice over his earphones. "What?" "That's right, lose all weapons now to lighten you up for a little more speed, then maximum speed to these coordinates, do you understand?" The pilot responded simply by saying "yes" as he let fly a million or so dollars worth of rockets.

Patrick was given a cell phone from one of the police that came to clear the landing area. As he spoke with Neil the Apache came in low and fast landing as though it were a hot LZ. Beth looked at her husband and wondered for the first time in years what her husband did that warranted this. The Apache picked up Patrick and left its navigator looking up at them as they flew away. He was then guided to a police cruiser. "What's all this about?" an officer asked the navigator as he still looked at the Apache becoming smaller and smaller in the sky. All he could do was shrug "I have no idea."

Patrick found himself listening to General Neil in the helmet. "How much time?" Neil responded with "23 minutes." The captain chimed in "It's going to take us just about 20 minutes to get to these coordinates even at top speed." General Neil then came over the radio "Captain; you are to exceed your maximum speed." "Sir that may damage this craft." The captain responded. "No captain, it will burn out your motor and that is an order, you got me, Captain." Neil was using his I am a General and you will not question me again voice. "Yes, sir." The captain responded as he pushed the throttle into the red and realized, whatever this man was doing, he had just been ordered to destroy a 14.5 million dollar craft to gain about 8 minutes.

As the craft landed with the engine smoking and sputtering, a sergeant came running up, "Mr. Pierce, please come with me." Patrick knew where he was going already and raced to the elevator. What seemed an eternity finally ended as the elevator stopped, Patrick raced out of the elevator to the prototype, and did a quick check. General Neil was watching the last wires being connected; "you're on Pat." Patrick jumped over a console to get to the terminal, he yelled out "time!" "Two minutes" someone yelled. Patrick typed as it began to come online, error came up. Patrick began typing again as the room fell silent. One minute left as Patrick glanced at a timer. Patrick found himself racing across the keyboard, 20 seconds, as he punched the keys. Finally the equipment came online and the wormhole began collapsing with 3.8 seconds left on the clock. The room let loose with a howl of delight. General Neil put his finger in one ear as he spoke into the red phone 'Mr. President, the situation is under control, yes sir." As Neil hung up the phone, he looked at Patrick and glowed. Patrick now had time to think of everything and felt his heart pounding in his chest. The smile he had was overshadowed by the thought of what could have just happened.

Over the next three hours the system was brought completely online and all the components for a second collapsing mechanism where ordered. The order to build another mechanism immediately had already been given.

Patrick smiled at Shannon as he walked into Neil's office. "Andy that was too close." "Well you know it's only a reprieve." Neil responded. Patrick cocked his head and ferruled his eyebrows. "Pat, you have heard of the fleet, haven't you?" Neil looked at Patrick with a slight cock of his head. Patrick shook his head slowly "no". "Well, I shouldn't tell you this but the Nyktarians also told us that if the wormholes could be blocked for over 50 years, then the Chiria would build a fleet and transport the invasion force via this fleet. Pat it's been 50 years, and we have about 50 years left until this fleet will be here." Patrick felt numb. "Why wasn't I told this?" Patrick asked quietly. "Why would you be?" Neil said slowly in a voice reserved for stupid questions. Patrick took a deep breath and finally asked, "So what are we doing about this fleet?" Andrew looked at his friend; his face was as stone as he started "Pat, we aren't doing anything." The silence was crushing. Neil finally continued "it costs too much and it isn't politically good for elections and all that." Patrick slumped into a chair; he felt he needed to hear a better answer even though there was none, "what are we doing here then?"

CHAPTER XI
The politicians don't always make good choices

Even though Patrick was a hero, Presidential citation and all, he walked around in a daze for the next week. The thought of a fleet seemed to kick him harder then any boot could. It was Neil that finally came to him in a good mood. "Pat I have some news." Neil was smiling from ear to ear. "Next month I am going to New York for a United Nations Security Counsel meeting to inform them of the threat." Now Patrick came alive, he breathed deeply and let out a long breath "finally". The next week Patrick went over everything with Andy, trying to prepare him for all the questions that were sure to come up. "My God Andy, this could mean the end to war on earth, all the resources would be going to countering the Chiria. This could very easily be the beginning of a new time on earth." Neil looked at him "well I'll be happy with a security arrangement or even some training together, you know just acknowledge the threat." Patrick's eyes bore through Andy, "I guess that would be a good start, but we are running out of time." As Andy left for the airport, Patrick felt like a young boy again, with infinite possibility before him, and the world.

The two weeks that Neil was away went by so slowly for Patrick. Even Beth knew Andy's trip was important but Pat had never been this excited and anxious before. The morning Neil was due back Patrick could hardly contain himself. General

Neil should have been back from New York; maybe now a defense plan would begin to take shape. The long ride down the elevator seemed to take twice as long as usual before Sergeant Davis finally opened the elevator doors. Patrick took long strides, almost running to Neil's door. Shannon, the secretary smiled and pushed a button "Patrick's here sir." When there was no response, she just shrugged "why don't you just go in, he seemed a bit down when he came in and maybe you can cheer him up." A bit down? Patrick thought that couldn't be good. As the doors swung open Patrick almost fell on himself in pure disbelief. Never had the General ever been anything but a professional soldier, until now.

"General" Patrick said when the smell of schnapps struck his nose like a slap to his face. General Neil lay semi-conscious on his desk, Patrick knew he was drunk. He allowed the door to shut behind him as he walked two steps into the room, then turned and clicked the lights on. "My God, why?" Neil looked at Patrick, "Pat, my friend, do you know that I always liked you." Oh great, a mushy drunk, thought Patrick.

Patrick turned on the intercom, "Shannon, me and the General will be working over, please tell our wives, and we don't wish to be disturbed O.K." Shannon's voice came back a moment later "of course sir." Patrick turned on the coffeepot; it was going to be a long night.

Neil was a good man and had been a great soldier, but as he told Patrick all the things he had done, some never where "published", assassinations, coups, and even small wars that no one ever knew of the American involvement in. Patrick could sense the desperation in his voice. "Pat, do you know that we only have about 50 years before that fleet will reach us?" Patrick set another cup of coffee down in front of the General. "Yea I know." Neil swung his head around and looked right at Patrick. "You know what we know about them?" Pat sat down next to his friend, "not really Neil, why?" "Pat, we know absolutely nothing, zip, zilch, zero. We don't even know how to stop them or whether we even could." Patrick swallowed hard, hard enough for Neil to see, taking another sip of his coffee Neil continued. "You should be scared, because you want to know what the UN is going to do about it?" No, no, no, Patrick thought I don't want to know let me just sleep easy at night OK, but a meek "what" escaped his lips. "Nothing, but cut my budget and shut down the number two site." Now it was Patrick's turn "no, they can't do that!" Neil slowly nodded his head up and down. "Oh yes they can, site one will be updated, made redundant and by treaty no Nuke's will be pointed here and whenever the Chiria do attack, everyone agrees to help fight, but until then no other military cooperation is planned at this time." As an afterthought General Neil leaned over "Oh we will also get our own power generator in here and about 2 years worth of fuel, completely self sufficient. As for the approaching fleet, well next year the UN will have another meeting." Neil slumped his shoulders as he rolled his eyes. "Pat, the meeting was a joke. All very low level personnel and I'm not invited. They're blowing it off, way too expensive for this political climate and to get the funds, well a lot of people would have to be told, and you know that would just frighten people." Neil then fell silent. Looking at the clock "I should get home, Pat. Sorry to be so down." "I don't think we could be anything but, Andy." Patrick responded.

Patrick came through the bedroom door and Beth could tell all was not well. "What's wrong love?" Patrick just bent over and kissed her on the top of the head, wrapped his arms around her and just stayed there all night. When he closed his eyes he would think of the horror that awaited the world, no sleep came this night only night mares.

As the alarm sounded Patrick pushed the snooze button, something he almost never did, and laid back down. His head hurt as he thought about everything. Patrick closed his eyes; his head hurt too much, so he finally rolled out of bed and without any feeling began to get ready for the day ahead. He felt like a zombie, just going through the motions.

As Patrick walked into the old building, he could already see the sergeant looking beyond him, as though something terrible had happened. Patrick approached the sergeant just as he looked up from the desk. "Sir, have you heard?" "Heard what sergeant?" Patrick responded without much of his usual good will. "Sir, ah, well, the General, sir he, sir I am sorry but General Neil shot and killed himself last night." Patrick just stood there, unable to move. "This couldn't be, not Andy" Patrick thought. "Sir, are you alright? Sir?" Patrick finally blinked and looked at the sergeant, he found no words, and he just raised his arm and slowly sank into a chair almost falling on the floor. Patrick stayed there for a few minutes, until he could stand again. When he could finally talk, he forced the words out "I can't work today, O.K. call me in ill." The sergeant just nodded, everyone knew they were tight so the sergeant had already received instructions that if Mr. Pierce wanted to work, he would not be allowed.

The next two days were a living nightmare. Beth and Joshua were terribly shaken. All the while Patrick looked at Andrew's family and knew why he did this and couldn't tell them or Beth or anyone for that matter, he had to carry this cross alone, and a terribly heavy cross it was. Patrick sat down with pen and paper, slowly he began to write. When he was finished, he sealed the envelope and put it in his coat pocket. Patrick had never even considered resigning, until now. He couldn't go on knowing that all this was for nothing, but how could he go somewhere else knowing that no matter what he did it would be in vain. 50 years just didn't seem that long anymore. Joshua came up "Dad". Patrick turned and forced a smile "hey, son what's up?" "Could you loan me the car?" "Sure." Patrick just couldn't see where it would hurt. That is when Patrick could take no more. Waiting for Joshua to leave the room Patrick then put his head down; the tears came streaming down his face as he sobbed for the loss of his friend, and the loss of innocents, Patrick knew too much to be happy now.

Patrick met General Johnson in the afternoon. Patrick had barely entered his office when he was confronted by the new General. "I know you and General Neil were friends. Well I don't think any civilians should be here, but I have to tolerate you and your department. So I recommend we just stay out of each others way OK." Patrick stared at Andrew's replacement, all spit and polish, a ton of medals but none for combat. "Oh great, a paper pusher" Patrick thought. "We work better together." Patrick tried to explain but was cut off "Well" General Johnson began "I don't think so, and I am in charge here so" as he shooed Patrick with his hand "why don't you run along." Patrick shook his head and left. "Oh this is great." He reached into his pocket and felt his resignation more tempting now then ever before. Patrick would put his hand on the letter more today, with the thought of leaving almost overwhelming him. He would never know why he didn't pull it out, only that he didn't that day. As Patrick drove toward home, he pulled into a park and shut off the car. Just sitting there, Patrick made his decision; he could not remain there and do nothing. So, first thing tomorrow morning, Patrick decided he would submit his resignation letter.

CHAPTER XII
Some decisions are harder then others

Patrick stepped through the door and found Beth sitting at the kitchen table, tears in her eyes. She looked up at him and slowly handed him the letter, unopened, from General Neil, marked private. He must have mailed it the night he died. Patrick starred at it for a long time. Finally he walked into the den, shut the door, and opened the letter.

Pat,

I know I am being replaced, to damned vocal at the UN. I can't go anywhere when I know that no matter what, it's useless. I don't know what to tell you, but do something. The world must know before it's too late. Here is a code, it isn't supposed to exist. This code overrides everything at the site. Only I know of its existence, having friends comes in handy and I guess once a spook always a spook, trust no one! XXX58973AA omega, this overrides everything at the base, even presidential codes. I know you will save this planet somehow. I am so sorry I failed, so I leave everything in your hands. I know if I had stayed, my debriefing would have revealed this code. I'm too damn honest in those matters. This way, only you have the code.

Good luck my friend,

Andy

Patrick slumped down; after a long while Beth knocked on the door. As she entered, she looked at him so intently that he could feel her ask without asking. Patrick looked into her gaze.

He began to speak, rethought it and then lowered his gaze. How could he explain this or even where could he begin.

The next three days were the longest of his life. The burden on his shoulders bore down like a load of bricks that he couldn't lay aside. One day while Patrick was at his console a wormhole began to emerge. As he zeroed in on the location Patrick suddenly stopped. The burden was gone from his shoulders and as though a light had been turned on Patrick breathed easily for the first time in days. Patrick realized where he was, did a quick look around, seeing only one or two people were looking his way yet and as Patrick began collapsing the wormhole they went back to work. Wormholes were very frequent and Patrick and his team logged them and collapsed them all the time so Patrick knew what and how he must proceed.

When he came through the door that evening Patrick kissed Beth and for the first time since Andy's death, was full of life. "What was gotten into you?" Beth asked in bewilderment. "I feel great and I know what I'm doing finally." "Well it's good to have you back, finally." Beth smiled at him as she emphasized the word finally. Patrick breathed deeply "Well I just had to make a really hard decision but now that I have made the decision I feel great. Oh by the way I am working midnight Monday night, so I thought Sunday," swaying his head and moving as if to a song, "Dinner, movie, Joshua to that arcade place, just a family day out. What do you say?" Beth had to laugh; she hadn't seen Pat this animated in a long time "OK" she said with a half smile of her own.

The weekend saw Patrick suck the marrow of life from every second, as though it may be his last. Saturday proved to be a family day of fun with Patrick starting a popcorn fight with Joshua at the movie. They almost got kicked out. When they arrived home it was almost 2am and everyone headed to bed. When Beth climbed into bed she looked at Patrick and smiled. "Now why are you in such a grand mood?" Patrick just moved ever so close to her until she could feel he was unclothed and obviously craving much more attention as he leaned over her and kissed her.

Patrick was up before Beth, already showered and dressed. "Up so soon?" Beth wearily asked. "Well I have the midnight shift and I also have some other things to do." Patrick stopped and looked long into Beth's eyes. Beth finally smiled and looked down feeling very girlish again. "I love you, you know?" Beth answered by just raising here eyes to meet his and smiling. Patrick stepped toward her and decided he could be a little late today as he climbed back into bed pretending not to hear Beth's groaning question of "what are you doing now?"

On his way out of the house, Patrick stepped into Joshua's bedroom, kissed the young man on the forehead. Joshua opened his eyes and blinked. "Oh I didn't mean to wake you." "It's ok dad." Came the response in a sleepy voice. "I love you son, and I hope you will always know how much." Joshua was still mostly asleep when he answered "I know." As he pulled the covers up to his neck and closed his eyes falling back into the land of slumber.

CHAPTER XIII
Some choices you can never take back

Patrick's day went as always. Johnson just stayed away until almost the end. "Mr. Pierce?" Patrick turned and forced a smile "yes general." In a cold voice he stated "come here." It was an order, as he walked into his office. Patrick took a deep breath as he stared after the General and thought how arrogant this man is. Patrick entered the office and saw the General almost look happy. "Oh no, what's wrong?" Patrick thought. "Yes general." Patrick stated in his most professional and unemotional voice he could muster. "Mr. Pierce, I have just been informed that your department is being phased out. You and your personnel are being replaced by military personnel, as it should have been in the first place." Patrick just stared as General Johnson gloated and with no meaning behind the words said, "I am sorry." then in a triumphant grin "It's effective as of the 15th of next month." Patrick turned and walked out. He knew of this plan being thought about, but he didn't think they would act on it like this. "Oh well, too late anyway." Patrick thought as he looked out at the brand new generator in the command center.

That night Patrick came in on the night shift as planned and sat down at the console. Nothing happened until 3:07am, when a wormhole began to open just south of the U.S. border in Mexico. Patrick looked over too the technician and then to the armed guard. Satisfied they were to far away to respond

Patrick then typed in the code, XXX58973AA omega. Patrick reached over to the execute key and paused. Patrick took a deep breath and pushed the key. "Patrick" the technician started to say, "My system froze up." Patrick looked over to him and very calmly stated, "Yes I know, I did it." Shock and then terror filled the man's face. "What? Why? How?" The words coming almost by themselves and growing in pitch as they where said. Patrick suddenly felt the impact to his head and fell out of his chair; the sergeant stood over him screaming "unlock the fucking computer!" With the muzzle of his rifle pointed directly at Patrick "you" "shut the fuck up and unlock the computer now asshole." The young man was both frightened and anxious. Patrick began again "if" "shut the fuck up." Patrick now screamed at the sergeant "if I die no one can close the hole." The sergeant looked at Patrick and then to the technician. The technician just shrugged, he didn't have a clue. The sergeant then told the technician "get over here, see if you can do anything." As the technician reached the console, he began typing. "I can't do a thing; there's a code access. Without it we're fucked." The sergeant now looked at Patrick "what's the fucking code you asshole." Now it was Patrick's turn, as he looked up Patrick then began to stand. Sergeant Edwards became even more tense, moving back a step. "Well now I am the only" Patrick emphasized the word only "Person that knows the code. Are you sure you want something to happen to me?" As sergeant Edwards swallowed and his eyes looked all around him as though searching for an answer. Patrick continued, "I am leaving this wormhole open for eight hours and then I will collapse it. You had better realize that unless you want it open forever I am the only one that can close it, so" Patrick paused and then screamed "stand down!" Edwards slowly lowered his rifle as he realized he could do nothing to

Patrick not yet anyway. Patrick looked at the console and then looked up, "30 minutes until the wormhole opens." Patrick then reached over to the red phone. It had never been used except for once, and never to report an opening, until now. As he lifted the receiver and heard the other end come online "Captain Greer." "Hello captain." Patrick's voice was very calm, as he reached up to his head and felt a bit of warm sticky goo were he had been hit "you better wake your superiors captain." The captain stuttered for a moment and then "what's going on?" "Captain I have entered a code that froze up the computer and a wormhole is going to open in about 30 minutes." "A code? What code, you entered what? Sir could you repeat that?" "Of course Captain, I have a code that locked up the site and I am leaving the wormhole open for eight hours, is that clearer captain?" "The code, sir." The captain demanded with a bit of a waver in his voice. "Captain, this is an active wormhole opening in 28 minutes." Captain Greer was quiet for a moment then "yes sir." as he hung up and started to call the rest of his command not sure he could even now believe what he had just been told. Three minutes later Patrick picked up the phone and found himself talking to General Johnson. "What in the hell is going on?" "General" Patrick began "I am allowing a wormhole to open and you need to alert the armed forces." "You what? Pierce, collapse that hole now." The general ranted. "General, I suggest you make the calls you need." As Patrick hung up the phone he had to smile, thinking how much he really hated that man.

When the red phone rang again Patrick just stared at it for a moment. Sergeant Edwards looked at him "Sir, the phone." Edwards was much more polite now. Patrick reached over and lifted the receiver. "Mr. Pierce, this is the President, what's going on?" "Well sir the long and the short of it is you decided to do nothing about this threat and I decided to bring it to the forefront, by allowing a wormhole to open for eight hours." "My God man you can't do this thing." "Sir you have already tried to override the computer and by now you know you can't or we wouldn't be talking. There is 13 minutes left until the wormhole opens I advise you go to a war footing and alert the military if you haven't already. Oh you may also want to call on our allies." Patrick added as an afterthought. "I'll nuke 'em." The President threatened. "Sir you could try, but you don't have the coordinates and that leaves you unable to nuke 'em, sir." The President then tried to reason or plead whichever would work, "Please don't do this." "Sir" Patrick spoke calmly almost as though to a child "you have precious little time." "Mr. Pierce, we will broadcast the threat, increase military cooperation, anything you ask, just don't do this." "Sir, I know that anything you say to me now is not considered something you have to follow through on, I am considered a lunatic and you can break any promise you make without any loss of conscience. Anything you broadcast can be withdrawn. This wasn't done on a whim, for I now believe there is no other way for the people of the world to be informed of this threat but to experience it." Patrick then hung up the phone and closed his eyes, seven minutes left until the hole opens, Patrick sighed, it was going to be a long seven minutes.

CHAPTER XIV
WAR

As the Chiria poured through the wormhole, they began spreading out in all directions. Even though only one hole was opened to earth, the Chiria brought a lot more troops through than anyone expected. Every estimate made for a wormhole opening believed that congestion at the wormhole entrance would delay their deployment somewhat. Eight hours was believed to require a major effort, but only one division was thought to be able to get through in that time. What no one knew was that when the Chiria finally had an opening to earth, they opened another wormhole for troop deployment. They opened a hole in front of their troops that exited to the entrance to the hole to earth, this way they could fly aircraft straight to earth one minute and shift holes so as to send infantry or armor the next moment, from all over their planet. No one ever guessed they would do this and so as eight hours went by more troops, aircraft and armor than were thought possible came to an unsuspecting earth.

The first casualties were families that had no warning, and then local Mexican police arrived and found themselves utterly outmatched. The local radio stations were able to report only of a disturbance, not knowing that this would be known as the point of death from this time on. The Chiria also poured through aircraft in flight to take to the skies. Commercial planes were suddenly sent out of the sky, a burning mass of debris.

As the Chiria aircraft flew north, the United States was already mobilizing, and in an ironic twist, a British Squadron was training in Texas when the alert came. Five British Harriers' that where already in the sky fully armed for a training flight, found an enemy they couldn't identify. Air control quickly gave "Weapon's free fire at will." Major Thomas William Moore flew towards the blips on his screen, at missile range all five harriers fired, only to see the strange crafts veer and their missiles go harmlessly away. "Jamming?" It was more of a question then a statement that Major Moore heard over his headset. Suddenly two harriers vaporized. "Evade and switch to guns." For 27 seconds they danced in the sky, and then Major Moore saw his chance. Coming down 10,000 feet with Lt. Dunn as his wingman, he came on a Chiria craft. As his wingman burst into flames, Major Moore squeezed his trigger and let loose a long burst into the Chiria craft. He never heard his wingman die, so intent on his victim and when the Chiria craft burst into flames and smoke Major Moore let loose a growling howl of delight. The high pitched buzz sounded informing him of a radar lock on him. Instinctively he jerked the stick left hard, pushing the throttle full open. The g's pushed him back but the buzz stayed with him until he briefly heard metal on metal as his craft burst into a ball of fire and disintegrated. The first combat over United States soil wasn't with U.S. forces, but British and five earth craft to one Chiria craft would be the best ratio of the war, normally it would be about 10 to one.

The first Mexican military units found a humanoid covered in armor, with a helmet and dark glasslike face shield. As the Mexican's engaged, they soon found themselves being cut to ribbons. Hiding behind anything less then a brick wall was useless as the Chiria's rounds cut right threw them. As a soldier glanced down at the minor cut in his arm he smiled, then rolled his eyes into the back of his head and coughed, began drooling and then collapsed. It was found that even a minor scratch from a Chiria round proved fatal, some poison must be on their rounds. The Mexican's that did survive the first encounter relayed their failure to their superiors, which would spread the word to the world. Even in loosing the field though, valuable information was passed to those that would fight latter.

One drug lord in northern Mexico brought out a case of armor piercing rounds. The Chiria squad was cut in half, Rafael had never been anything but a thug, and now he put his talents to use as he began ambushing Chiria squads. He didn't have a lot of armor piercing rounds but with each small victory he gained more of the Chiria weapons. So it was that a small time drug enforcer would be the first to have even minor victories against the Chiria.

The Chiria butchered everyone caught near them as they flowed out of the wormhole for eight long hours. The air war was crushing as the ground was swarming with Chiria forces. As more armor piercing and Teflon coated bullets made there way to the front, the Chiria found their casualties growing. Earth tanks were found to be very susceptible to Chiria rounds as they went right through the armor, stopping our tanks cold. The Chiria also had tanks of their own. The Chiria tanks entered the battlefield to find that our anti-tank rockets would destroy them, at a high cost to us though.

CHAPTER XV
The first Heroes

The Cuban's were the first to land a battalion in Mexico. Colonel Rodriguez looked out at his men. They had dug and enforced their position. Colonel Rodriguez had 2,000 men under his command as the Chiria approached. "Colonel, we are ready." A young adjutant said. "I doubt that." Rodriguez responded as he looked out with his binoculars. "Chiria tanks and infantry." He said to no one in particular. When the Chiria came into the killing zone, Colonel Rodriguez gave the signal. The whole area erupted in fire and explosions. The Chiria tried to rally, but were forced back. Colonel Rodriguez then saw a group of 20 men rush toward a Chiria tank. Rapid gunfire dropped 7 but 13 men reached the tank. Six men jumped up on the Chiria vehicle and two promptly were shot off. Then as a hatch opened, the soldiers fired point blank, killing the Chiria tanker. The soldiers then pulled a cord and dropped a satchel charge inside. The soldiers began to run back to their lines as the tank spewed flames. Rounds tore through the soldiers five yards from their lines. As the last man fell, Colonel Rodriguez thought it ironic that the most advanced tank on the planet was destroyed not by some other high tech device, but by brave foot soldiers and a satchel charge.

When the Chiria finally fell back, Colonel Rodriguez knew this was the only chance he had. He ordered the tank quickly placed on a flatbed trailer, grabbed as many Chiria bodies and weapons that he could and shipped them south. They would go to the Mexican port of Tam Pico, where the Cubans wanted the equipment to go to Cuba, however the Mexican officials believed that the United States would be better able to research it so that is where they went. The equipment was loaded on a ship and sailed to New Orleans. From New Orleans they were sent to an American base for research.

Colonel Rodriguez looked at the stream of refugees. He had been ordered to retreat and all he could do was hope the stream of humans fleeing the fight would be shown mercy. Seven hours later, Colonel Rodriguez witnessed Chiria troops overtake the refugees. The Chiria butchered them, firing well into the night, killing men, women, and children, old and young. Colonel Rodriguez looked at the flames filling the sky. "I will never let this happen again." He swore.

China mobilized 500,000 troops and put them on every ship they could get. Private Woo looked out over the vast armada and thought this is truly a grand force. South America en-mass sent troops north to engage the Chiria in Mexico. Most of Europe would send troops to North America. NATO, so long expecting American forces to aid them in an emergency, found themselves sending their armies to the United States. Russia sent a massive army to Central America to fight in Mexico from the south.

Colonel Rodriguez peered out from his position. He had been reinforced and a lot of Mexican's had joined his force for a total of 8, 452 men and women under arms. He stared at the small piece of paper, then at the long line of refugees leaving Mexico City. "I can't abandon them, not again." Colonel Rodriguez thought of his family and knew, despite his orders, he couldn't leave this position. He turned to face his officers. "Reinforce your positions set all the mines, trip wires, everything. Gentlemen, we will not leave them to those butchers." Cocking his head toward the refugees. His officers quickly understood, and final letters were written and sent south to hopefully, find their loved ones and say goodbye. The Chiria reached Colonel Rodriguez's position late in the night. For six long days, it's said; the sound of battle could be heard before silence fell on the position. After the war a statue would be erected there and its said that Colonel Rodriguez's name would be said for the protection of refugees everywhere. Cuba had the first world wide hero that was mourned by every nation. Hundreds of thousands were able to make it south because of their sacrifice.

CHAPTER XVI
War is Hell

As the Chiria crossed into the U.S. they found stiff resistance. At first the Chiria crushed everyone in they're path. Entire towns were butchered; no prisoners were known to have been taken. American M-1 tanks found Chiria infantry rounds went right through their armor. If, however, if our tanks were close enough they could destroy the Chiria tanks also. Valleys, cliffs, everything that could be used for cover and to get our tanks closer was, even though the slaughter continued. As the Chiria reached San Diego, they were stopped by not the army or the police, but the local gangs that came out to fight. These young men and women were not disciplined, but they slowed the Chiria's progress, as the city was laid waste. It was enough for the moment.

Texas was overrun and some say it was as though a fire swept through the whole of the Lone Star State and burned everything. Over 90% of the state's population was killed and, as European forces reached America, they were quickly put into the fight. French command of New Orleans was swift and well determined. The Mississippi proved a great natural barrier, but north the Chiria swept up to the Canadian border before being stopped. The Rocky Mountains stopped them from overrunning California, and the Chinese landed in San Francisco to march south to Los Angeles, were the Chiria meet them head on.

Private Woo's battalion came to the battle naive and full of itself. Woo soon found his friends cut down in rows. As the Chiria advanced, the Chinese fell back, but here the fortunes of war changed. The Chinese had satchel charges and as the Chiria cut down the Chinese tanks, the infantry took satchel charges and blew up Chiria tanks. As some of the Chinese fell with the satchel charges still on their backs the satchel charges were detonated remotely as the Chiria advanced, with the Chinese still wearing the charged packs. This was most repulsive as wounded were left in order to trap the Chiria, but in war you use what works. The Chinese would then send out troops with charges, and if they reached the Chiria great, if not then the charges were remote detonated as the Chiria advanced, either way the Chinese killed Chiria troops. Los Angeles would be held. In 5 days of fighting though, the Chinese lost 348,921 dead. At the peak of the war the Chinese sent one million troops a week, and never until the very end did they have more then 400,000 troops available. The blood poured into the ground of southern California.

The Russians, Africans, and South/Central American forces first engaged the Chiria in mass just about 200 miles north of the southern boarder of Mexico. They were pushed back and back and back. The combined Russian lead force was pushed all the way back to the Panama Canal. That is where it was finally said 'no further". "No further" became the cry, and for six months the Panama Canal ran red with all the blood that poured forth. The combined force did stop the Chiria, but at a cost so high they could only hold for the time being while training more troops to come to the blood fields.

CHAPTER XVII
One person can make a difference

The old American smiled. He had been hunting before, but never like this. He knew he liked the 20 rounds of armor piercing bullets he had, even though they were illegal, he kept them around. Now he looked at the Chiria column and knew it was a good thing to have. He aimed his rifle, over the course of the years he had been hunting 27 years and not in over 25 years had he ever missed his prey. As he squeezed the trigger, he felt the powerful rock of the rifle and saw the Chiria spin and fall. The old man grunted, "I thought they would bleed green." as a bright almost florescent red/ orange spewed out of the Chiria soldier. The old man slowly crawled away, to await them down the road. This scene would play itself out all over the occupied area. The "soldiers" were mostly a rag tag bunch of people that came together and would make a difference.

General Johnson looked at Patrick. "I would like nothing better than to shoot you right now, but" Johnson gritted his teeth as he was forced to admit "you know too fucking much about this system and we need you to keep on collapsing the wormholes, but you will give me the code right now." Patrick looked up at the general; "first I need to see a news flash on CNN about the fleet." General Johnson looked about quickly as a number of technicians and security personnel froze, now staring intently at the two of them. Painfully aware that

Patrick was not authorized to know about the fleet the general responded slowly "let's take this into my office." Now Patrick did scream "No! The damn fleet, you know, what? No one here knows about the fleet?" Everyone in the command center was now looking at them. General Johnson crossed his arms and just glared at Patrick. "The fleet, its time to tell everyone, and I mean everyone about the fleet!" As General Johnson stood there Patrick reached over and picked up the red phone. "Yes there will be a news flash about the fleet; I am too tired to play these damn games, not right now." Patrick hung up the phone and looked at one of the technicians. "Turn on that TV to CNN." As he waited for the news flash Patrick showed little of the apprehension he felt. Finally, after about ten minutes, the program was interrupted and the breaking story about how in approximately 50 more years the Chiria fleet was expected and as of this date nothing had been done to prepare for this.

Patrick sat quietly for a few minutes before finally moving to the console. As he typed the code into the computer he knew that one-day he would have to account for what he had done. "General, the code is now deleted, the system is yours." General Johnson snapped "you're under arrest, corporal would you get this piece of shit out of here." "Sir" it was one of the technicians, about 25, Patrick thought his name was John. "Patrick's the only one who can multi-task the targeting system." He paused and took a deep breath "We really do need him or we will have another wormhole open up." "Fine!" Johnson snapped after a long moment of silence, looking right at the corporal "stay with him." General Johnson then turned and stormed out.

Patrick proved quite the diplomat. He couldn't be arrested because he knew too much of how to operate the equipment, but no one, especially the general, wanted him there, so they just kept him. As fuel was brought into the site, word came that the war was going badly. Already casualties were high, and retreat was the norm. Beth wrote Patrick to tell him that Joshua had enlisted, and she had volunteered for a field hospital unit with the Red Cross. Patrick felt overwhelmed; the only thing said to her was that he was needed for the war effort. Even so, Patrick knew it was him, and him alone that had placed his loving wife and his precious son in harms way. "How could you ever justify this?" Patrick thought to himself.

Corporal Woo's company advanced on the Chiria. With the most massive assault of the war the Chinese were launching what was hoped would be a great advance. As the Chiria fell back, optimism was high. That is until a massive Chiria counter attack came from the east and cut off 257,000 troops. The Chinese tried to break free of the trap but soon found it impossible. The Chinese high command's reserves stabilized the line, but couldn't get to the trapped men. Corporal Woo's company looked more like a platoon as he sat eating his rations. Everyone was quiet, they all knew they were trapped and would probably die. After three weeks of heavy fighting, the Chinese General knew he couldn't get back to his lines, and the Chiria didn't take prisoners. So, with his staff, it was decided, an all out attack, not to the north, but east where the Chiria didn't have as much armor. They could do nothing, nothing but kill as many Chiria as possible. Corporal Woo lined up with his men for the assault. The north, south, and west had been all but abandoned. It was to the east that they attacked and the Chiria were caught off guard. As the Chinese attacked so did the Chiria, and the pocket disintegrated. Woo ran to the Chiria line's firing and tripping, getting up and firing again. As he jumped into a trench he realized it was a hand to hand fight, which the Chinese were winning until some Chiria just sprayed their weapons, killing Chinese, Chiria, and anything in their way. Woo felt a massive fire in his shoulder as he was knocked to the ground. Looking at his shoulder and seeing blood just before loosing consciousness.

Woo slowly opened his eyes to massive amounts of dead, Chiria, Chinese, Friends, and enemies everywhere. Only Chiria troops were moving though.

Woo thought it odd that if the Chiria rounds were poisoned and he had been hit he should be dead. When he looked at his shoulder he realized it was a 7.62 round. The thought was ironically funny, friendly fire saved his life. As night fell Woo slowly got up and made his way back to his lines. Only 273 men of the initial attack made it back. Even so, the Chiria had lost a lot and the offensive was classified as a success, just not to the dead.

General Johnson scanned to the east, and saw the advancing Chiria, and then turned to the southwest to view the tankers. They had the badly needed fuel the site would be using; it was five years worth. Hopefully it wouldn't all be needed, but the sooner it was in the underground fuel tanks the better. Five years worth of food and water and whole truckloads of cards, chess, smokes, toilet paper, and popcorn where already in the site. The fuel was hard to get though, everyone wanted it. As General Johnson looked at the tankers suddenly two Chiria fighters came over the hills from seemingly nowhere, swooping down on the tankers, "No!" Screamed Johnson as a massive fireball filled the sky followed by the ear-piercing boom a few seconds later. Johnson grabbed his head in his hands screaming "Shit! Shit! Shit!" Turning to a captain "find out how much fuel we have!" Then General Johnson ran to the site himself.

"Mr. Pierce, do you have those plans?" Patrick looked

up from his desk, reached into a pile of papers and retrieved a set of schematic drawings of the collapsing mechanism. General Johnson snatched them up and raced to the elevator, pressing the button and stepped back, then reached forward and pressed the button again. Finally the doors opened and the general almost jumped in and then the doors closed.General Johnson frantically was calling a sergeant to him as he finished writing.

"Sir the site has a maximum of one years worth of fuel, no more. The rest was destroyed. Here are the diagrams for building a collapsing mechanism. Good luck."

He then signed the letter "General Johnson". Placing the letter in a brown leather diplomatic pouch he then closed and sealed it. "Take your squad and get this pouch to General O'Tool, he is in the regional command center. Now go." As Johnson looked at the four men climbing into the hummer and speed away he slowly turned his attention to the approaching Chiria.

When the Chiria came closer, General Johnson's troops fell back and ambushed as planned, but even so their well-prepared positions were still overrun. General Johnson crouched in the hall of the site as he heard the approaching Chiria. Slowly and methodically Johnson connected the last wire and as he saw three of his soldiers cut to pieces in the connecting hall he twisted the handle. The building disintegrated in the explosion, crumbling down on the entry to the site, burying the facility in what was hoped would be its anonymity and its safety.

The sergeant drove like a madman. He came up over a hill and right into a Chiria patrol. Both the Chiria and the squad of men opened fire. Three Chiria fell and two humans screamed out and then fell silent as the hummer's engine steamed and shrieked due to the hits and then slammed into a tree. A corporal went crashing through the windshield; the sergeant unbuckled his seatbelt, brushed the blood away from his eyes, grabbed the brown leather satchel and ran from the vehicle. He only made it about 20 yards before being cut down. The Chiria looked at his body and walked away, never even giving the diplomatic pouch a second glance, as the sergeant's blood slowly flowed over it.

Captain Woo looked at his men. He had heard that only 30 soldiers, one being himself, were still alive from the original 500,000 deployed. Woo actually thought 30 rather high. "Captain." A young, oh so young man thought Captain Woo, messenger "sir, the general would like to see you." Woo just barely nodded as the young boy saluted, turned and walked away. Woo didn't move for a moment, and then leaned forward, took his rifle, officers had pistols but old habits are hard to break and Woo had kept his rifle, and started off to the general's tent. The General was a scared looking man. He had been a good lieutenant but now he had seen to much death and sent to many men on too many one-way missions. He was burned out. Even so the General waved Captain Woo over with a shaking hand, slowly inhaling the cigarette. "Woo" the Generals voice was almost pleading, "Would you take your men, fly into Mexico to assist a rebel attack." Woo knew this General wouldn't last, he was already cracking. "Oh well, just one more General" Thought Woo. "Yes Sir." Woo then turned to an adjutant that gave the details.

For eleven months 23 days and 17 hours Captain Woo would lead his troops behind the Chiria lines, receiving supplies sporadically at best but at least he was out of the butcher's fields, as the Chinese front was called.

As Captain Woo reached allied lines in California, his first duty was to report what he and his men had discovered. Captain Woo's report was quickly sent up the chain of command, all the way to New York and the United Nations.

CHAPTER XVIII
The light at the end of the tunnel

Gentlemen" began the Chinese delegate "this information was brought to us only seven days ago." Waiting for emphasis, she then continued "the Chiria has utilized two major facilities. The first is a hospital in Mexico City. It appears as though the Chiria are cloning their soldiers from this facility, or at least some form of cloning technology. The second is a Ford Motor Company plant that is producing armor, tanks, and rounds for their troops." The delegates talked for hours and the generals where briefed and the plans laid out.

With the entire cruise missile fleet of the world came every bomber of all the air forces of the world. Russian, British, and American aircraft, never before had so many planes embarked to destroy two small sites. Even the Chiria defenses were overwhelmed, but at a substantial cost. The cruise missiles lit up the night and set the world aflame, nuclear weapons were found to give themselves away with high radiation levels that the Chiria quickly zeroed in on and destroyed. The return flight was not seen by most of the aircrews that flew into the nightmare flight of this single evening. 97% of the world's bomber fleet lay smoldering on the ground when the mission was declared a success, only not by the widows, orphans, and weeping mothers that were left after the raid.

The offensive was going very slow. "What the hell did

they expect?" Thought Sergeant Manning. Attacking in the California Mountains was stupid. Manning then saw something and quickly dropped to the ground, followed rapidly by his squad. Having seen no movement he slowly sat up, and then kneeled and slowly stood. As he walked to the old hummer he looked at the dead soldiers. Just another bunch of dead men, killed maybe just over a year ago. "That's odd" said a private "no driver." Sergeant Manning looked up and saw another body about 30 yards away. As Manning walked up to the dead man his eyes fell on a brown leather case, a diplomatic pouch. For a few seconds he just stood there looking at the pouch. Slowly he reached down and picked up the pouch, it was full of holes and covered in dried blood. The seal was intact and Sergeant Manning knew enough to know that this needed to get to someone higher up then him.

The United Nations diplomats listened as the general spoke of the success of the missile and bomber attack. An aide ran up to one of the generals; quick hurried words were then exchanged. Finally the general speaking to the diplomats stopped, "is there something we should know?" The aid stepped away as General Ostiwich stood, cleared his throat and began "Gentlemen, Ladies, as you all know the site was buried a year and three months ago. We believed that five years worth of supplies had been placed in the site. We now know that this is not true." Worried looks crossed everyone's faces as twenty voices began speaking at the same time. "Order! Order! We must have order." General Ostiwich shouted, as the room slowly grew quiet. Holding up the bloody, holed brown leather case "this was recovered three days ago. Inside we have a letter from General Johnson stating that there is only one years worth of fuel that made it to the site. Ladies and Gentlemen, we are already past one year." Ostiwich remained silent for a moment to allow this to sink in. "We do not know how they are still operating, or even if they are still operating, except that no further wormhole has opened so far." Our assault in California toward the site is going nowhere. The Chiria defenses are too well established in the mountains."

CHAPTER XIX
Ingenuity

Patrick moved the pawn, "check." The site was dark, lit only by two battery operated lamps. A high piercing sound suddenly shrieked. Patrick looked at his computer, turning one switch and then another "OK we've got one." The generator was supposed to be run all the time but with so little fuel, Patrick had it shut down. The generator was run only when a wormhole needed to be collapsed and at that time they also charged the batteries. When there was no wormhole, battery power only was used to monitor for them. By doing this the fuel had lasted a lot longer then anyone thought, but they still only had two maybe three months left. With all this time though Patrick had become very good at chess. The military thought of everything, they had games, and cards, and popcorn. The only problem was that everyone used the microwave oven. With the increased use, breakfast lunch and dinner, the machine only lasted two months. Of course there were no spare microwaves packed away. They managed to rework the thing once, but it only lasted another month. After that the food was all cold, but even worse was that they had five years worth of popcorn stored in one of the rooms. All the popcorn was micro-wave able, so all anyone could do was look at the popcorn and wish they could try some. Patrick really missed popcorn; not that he liked it that much before, just that he couldn't have it now.

"The Chiria haven't made any major offensives since about one month after the bomber and missile attack." The young officer was explaining to the United Nations Military Command. "Our reports inside the occupied zone indicate that a lot of posts have been abandoned and the troops sent to the front. The colonel stopped, breathed deeply and continued "We believe the Chiria are hollow. To put it simply, our attack was more effective then we ever dreamed. The front lines are still manned but if we get behind their lines we should find little resistance." A Russian general broke in "and if you are wrong?" The colonel looked directly at the general and with a stone cold face answered solemnly. "We will send about a million soldiers to their deaths." The silence fell on the room like a weight around the necks of everyone there. Finally the colonel continued "and if we do nothing, soon, another wormhole will open and the human race will cease to exist."

The Chinese continued heavy pressure in the San Diego area. The NATO forces of America and Europe organized in San Francisco and set sail. Russia and her allies grouped in Cuba. The Russian fleet sailed a half a day after the NATO force. NATO forces hit the West Coast of Mexico two hours after the Russian force had begun landing on the East Coast of Mexico. As the Russians fought their way south the NATO force turned north. Even being so massively undermanned the Chiria gave very little ground. As their lines collapsed the Chiria began dying in place. They never knew there was such things as surrender, and would never even consider it if they did know. The UN forces found the Chiria would fight to the end, even going hand to hand when all hope was gone to them.

With the American's approaching, the Chinese could see the end for the Chiria. The Chiria knew they could not stop the American forces coming from the south. So the Chiria launched an assault on the Chinese. It made sense to the Chiria, and very few others. Colonel Woo knew his brigade was in trouble as he watched the forces to his right collapse. Woo ordered a retreat to find that Chiria forces had been airlifted to the north, cutting them and most of the Chinese, off. Woo managed to keep most of his brigade intact as he fell back. When the ocean greeted him, he knew he needed to find killing ground. Woo found a series of hills and quickly began placing his troops in a defensive ring around the hills. Woo looked out onto the beach, at the hundreds of support troops running and sometimes milling about. "Fuck 'em." Woo thought "I can't even keep my men safe; this is going to be bloody." Woo turned to a captain "Set up all around the hill, the Chiria will come up the beach, prepare accordingly." The captain looked at the hundreds of men on the beach, realizing they were being considered a loss, "yes sir." And went about his work, what did he care.

Colonel Woo looked out into the black of night. As he peered out he could see the tracers and flashes getting closer. When behind him burst into fire, shouting and screams. Woo raced to the other side of the hill, lifted a flare gun into the air and fired. The coast lit up in a green glow, the Chiria were everywhere and they began firing. Colonel Woo's troops were in shock at their presence but quickly opened up. The Chinese mixed in with the Chiria would just have a bad day.

As the Americans approached the stink of death filled the air. They said this was one of the last Chinese positions to hold. As the troops approached the beach, the dead were everywhere. Chiria, Chinese, and those that were too badly mangled to even tell. Nothing moved, as though the two armies had fought themselves to death. One lone figure sat on a hill where even more dead seemed to be than anywhere else. A single soldier, from the 82nd airborne began walking toward the Chinese soldier. The airborne trooper knew what it was like to be the only one left from all those that parachuted with him. Woo looked up at the lone American walking toward him. Suddenly Woo started laughing. He could never tell you what was so funny. As the American came up to Woo he slowly knelt down and took him in his arms. Woo could never say when the laughter stopped or when the tears started. Woo looked out over all the dead through his tears and realized the American was crying with him. Woo reached up and held him tight. The one thought Woo had was "so this is victory." It felt hollow.

CHAPTER XX
What price victory

Patrick screamed out "mate." He was the best player but it was really good to beat the sergeant. He was an arrogant prick. "Quite, quite!" Some tech was screaming. As the site fell silent wondering what he heard. They faintly heard the sound of rocks and rubble being moved from the elevator shaft. The soldiers raced to get their weapons and take up their positions. Patrick dove behind a panel. The sergeant held out a 9mm. "If they're not ours." Patrick looked at the sergeant and then the handgun, hearing more rubble being moved Patrick reached out and took the pistol. He closed his eyes, swallowed and cocked the pistol. "Hello, is anyone in there?" The voice was faint but definitely an American accent. The sergeant screamed out before anyone else "how do we know who you are?" The voice boomed back "code word tora, tora, tora." Came the all-clear code. Everyone in the site screamed out in joy, Patrick remained silent. He knew what he had done, and that he would have to take responsibility for it. Patrick then looked at the pistol in his hand. For an instant Patrick looked into the shine of the firearm. Sergeant Rorke slapped Patrick on the shoulder and screamed "we made it." Patrick looked up at the young man. Slowly Patrick raised the pistol and then extended his hand and held the weapon out to the sergeant who only then realized what Patrick had been thinking. Rorke just took the pistol and stared, realizing what Patrick would now face.

As the site came back to full power and the lights were finally turned on Patrick was barely able to open his eyes. A captain came in and walked over to Patrick, placed one cuff on Patrick's wrist "you're under arrest." As he took Patrick's other hand and cuffed it.

The whole story had been told to the world, including Patrick's part. Patrick sat in his prison cell waiting to be transported to Geneva for trial, "your mail." A soldier said holding a whole box of mail. At first both Joshua and Beth wrote regularly, and then the letters changed. The news of Patrick's part in this war was made clear to them. Patrick read bitter words from Joshua, as he saw more of his fellow soldiers and friends killed. Beth was first hurt, then mad and then bewildered. Her last letter asked why, explained everything Patrick had thought, and asked why again. That's when the letter from the Army came along with the commander of a field hospital, explaining how Beth had been very brave as the Chiria overran the hospital. The "I'm sorry" wasn't very much help. Patrick sat crying as he realized his love was lost and he never could explain why he had done what he had. After Beth's death, Joshua wrote only one more letter, explaining that he never wanted to see or hear from him again.

"Mr. Patrick Pierce." The British Judge was saying "this court finds you guilty of crimes against humanity." There was no surprise in the verdict; the world needed someone to blame.

The months passed, with the procedures working they're way through, as an anxious world demanded blood, Patrick's blood. For all the dead in the one true world war required vengeance.

When Patrick finally was again standing before the court, he knew what would be said. As the words came ""you are sentenced to death." Patrick didn't even blink. When he walked back to his cell he looked at the captain and handed him a letter, "would you see that this is mailed?" The captain took the letter without a word, no one but his lawyer ever spoke to him.

Patrick's lawyer sat across from him explaining his appeal and all the papers that needed his signatures. Patrick finally looked up "why do you speak to me when no one else will?" His lawyer stopped writing, set his pen down and looked at Patrick. "Mr. Pierce, I speak to you because I have no choice, I am doing my best to represent you and defend you so my conscience is clear, and if I don't make any mistakes then" his voice turned acidic, his face curled in hate. "Then you won't have an appeal of inadequate representation so you will be executed for what you have done." He clenched his fist and then reached for his pen. "Let us get to work." Patrick half smiled leaned back in his chair "I refuse my appeal." His lawyer stopped and looked up. "What?" Patrick just continued "tell my son that my last request is to play a game of chess with him." Patrick then got up and knocked on the door. The soldier opened the door and Patrick looked back at his lawyer "I don't want to see you again outside of the courtroom, not that I am firing you, you will defend me as well as anyone, but I don't want to see you again, I see no use in it." Patrick then walked out of the room back to his cell.

Patrick heard the footfalls coming from the end of the corridor. When the door opened he knew it was Joshua immediately. Patrick smiled only a little, but his heart beat hard in his chest. Joshua's words were deliberate and angry as he explained how so many of his friends had died in that war. He would have been content never to hear or see him again. Patrick also listened as Joshua explained how he had placed a very high value on a man's last request. Even though Joshua felt he owed him nothing he had come. Patrick set up the board and the game began. Joshua had been an ok player, but Patrick soon saw that he was the better player, so his moves were very deliberate. The game went on for over an hour, and then two, as Joshua continued to tell his father how he blamed him for his friends, his youth, and most of all, his mother. Patrick then was ready and moved his queen. Joshua looked at the move and stated through clenched teeth "that was a stupid move." He then moved his bishop across the board and took Patrick's queen. Patrick then looked at his son. "Sometimes you must be willing, for the good of the whole, to sacrifice even your very best." Patrick then moved his castle over the board. "Checkmate." Joshua looked at the board and then clenched his teeth; in one swift movement he stood up and swung his arm across the board. Pieces flew everywhere. "Fuck you!" Joshua said as he went to leave the room.

Patrick's cell was opened and the soldier came in, "its time.' The soldier had never spoken to him before but seemed to get some pleasure from that one statement. Patrick stepped out into the corridor. With one forced step after another he slowly walked down the hall. Patrick had to look again, and then blinking looked yet again. Joshua stood still and then hesitatingly took a step forward. "Dad" he started slowly "I understand why you did what you did, and I want you to know" he stopped and licked his lips, " I love you dad." He then hugged him and stepped back. Finally understanding the sacrifice his father had made.

Patrick walked out into the field. The sun was shinning bright, with the international firing squad standing in a line. Patrick was lead to his spot and felt his hands tied to the post. As the soldiers took their position, Patrick closed his eyes and thought of his son. He did not think of him as he is now... "Ready", but rather at age 4. Running in from the yard..."Aim", with his baseball bat and glove. His blue hat cocked just to the side "Dad, do you want to play base..."Fire".

CHAPTER XXI
All good things

With the Chiria fleet approaching Pluto orbit, the commander listened to his adjutant's report. He looked out over the ships of his fleet. "We are approaching the Earth sir. There appears to be no effective defenses anywhere around the planet." The commander smiled thinking how pathetic these creatures are. He peered out over his fleet, when he then saw a dozen ships ripped apart by hundreds of mines.

"Enemy ships" one of his crew cried out. "Where?" The commander demanded. The crewmember looked at his screen and softly spoke the word "everywhere." The ships of the Earth Defense Directorate came out of well-prepared positions across the entire sky. The alien commander realized his entire fleet had sailed into a trap. The flames then licked up around the bridge of his ship; the deck plates buckled and broke. The alien ships were torn and burning as the Earth Defense Directorate Ship the Patrick O. Pierce led the human fleet to the most successful fleet engagement against the Chiria ever. Dedicated to the one man that performed the ultimate

...SACRIFICE...

Made in the USA
Lexington, KY
05 October 2017